The Red Book of wordplay Stories

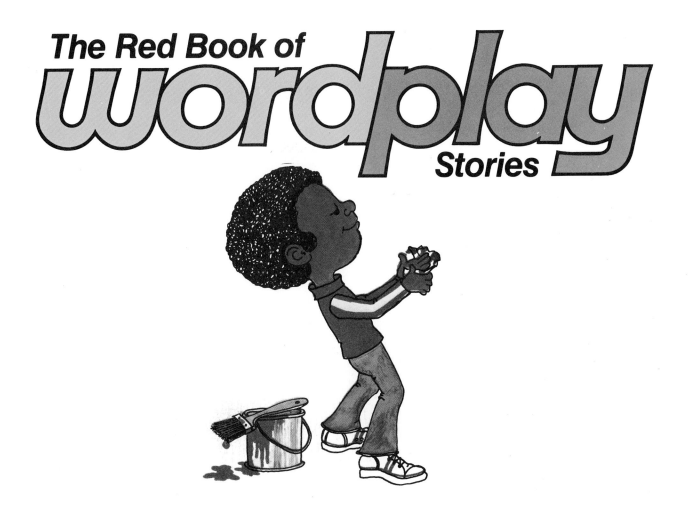

Written and Illustrated by

Susan Batko

Vocab Incorporated • Chicago

Consultant: **Ruth Hoffmeyer, M.A.**

Designer: Carol Becker

Cover Photographer: Daniel Czubak

Home Distributor:
The Southwestern Company
Franklin, Tenn. 37064

National School and Library Distributor:
Communacad
Wilton, Conn. 06897

Printed in the United States of America

Library of Congress Catalog Card Number: 77-70444

ISBN 0-918468-02-7

3   4   5   6   7   8   9   10   11   12   13   14   15   BB   86   85   84   83   82   81   80   79   78

Contents

The Bubble Gum

Bubble Maker

Harvey liked to work with tools.
He could follow directions for
making almost anything.
Sometimes he even made things that
he had thought up all by himself.

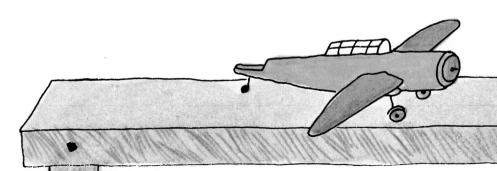

One day Harvey was busy in his
father's workshop.
As he worked, he chewed bubble
gum and blew bubbles.
One of the bubbles became very big.
It didn't break until it was
the same size as Harvey's head.

size

Harvey tried to blow more
bubbles just as big.
But each time he tried, he failed.

"I know what I'll do," he thought.
"I'll build a bubble maker—
a bubble maker that can blow great big
bubble gum bubbles one after another.
But how?"

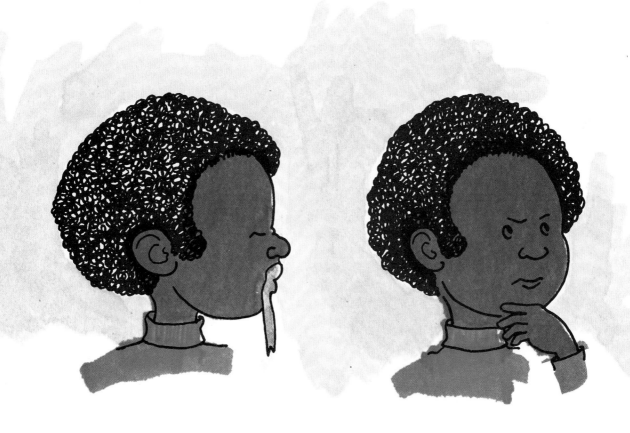

Harvey began to go through his
supply of wood and metal.

supply

11

He spread out the pieces on the floor.
There were wide boards,
narrow boards, small blocks, and
all kinds of old metal parts.

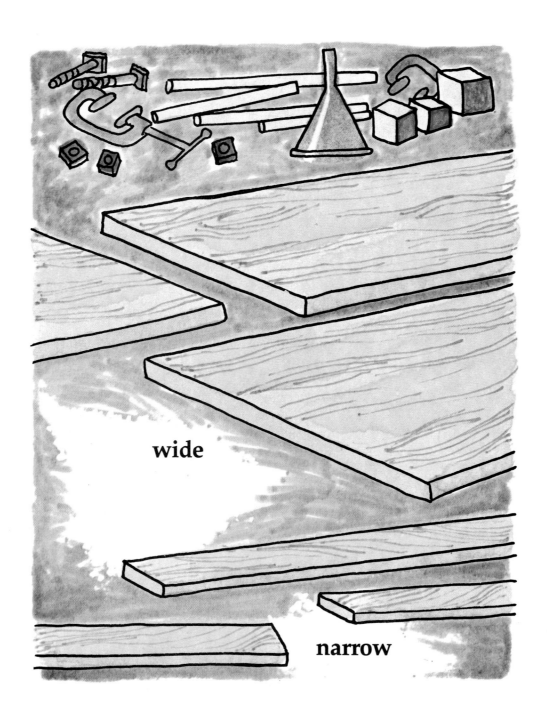

wide

narrow

"I think I know how to do it,"
he said to himself.
Then he began to nail some
of the boards together.

Harvey's big brother, Al, came into
the workshop and sat on the
edge of the workbench.
"What are you building now?" asked Al.

edge

15

"I'm building a bubble maker that will blow great big bubble gum bubbles one after another," replied Harvey.

replied

16

Al roared with laughter and said,
"That's crazy! It can't be done!"
He was still laughing as he went
out the door.

Later Harvey's little sister,
Nancy, came by.
"Why are you building this thing?"
Nancy asked.
"What is the purpose of it?"

"The purpose of it is to blow great big
bubble gum bubbles one after another,"
replied Harvey,
"the biggest bubble gum bubbles
in the world!"

purpose

BUBBLE
MAKER

That was the silliest thing Nancy
had ever heard.
And she ran to tell her friend.

Harvey locked the door and
went right on working.
He removed a nail from an old
piece of wood and pounded it into
the bubble maker.
It was coming along just fine.

removed

23

Before long everyone in the
neighborhood knew that Harvey
was building a bubble maker.
No one thought it would work.
But everyone began to wonder what it
would look like.

wonder

Many days went by.
Then at last Harvey finished the
bubble maker.
He couldn't wait to try it out.
He pulled it into the back yard where
there was lots of room.

finished

26

27

Just then Nancy, Al, and their friends joined him.

joined

29

It was the first time they had seen the
bubble maker, and they all began
laughing and talking.
"It looks like a circus wagon!"
"What's that, a clown's face?"
"Where are the bubbles?"

Before Harvey could reply,
they were all shouting,
"We want bubbles!
We want bubbles!"

Harvey's parents came out of the
house to see what was going on.
The neighbors heard the noise and
came running.

Suddenly the back yard was full of people.
Some of the children had to sit on
the fence so they could get
a view of the bubble maker.
It was fun to look at.
But would it work?

34

view

35

Harvey stepped into the crowd and
began to pass out his supply of bubble gum.
"As long as you're here,
you may as well help!" he shouted.
"Everyone start chewing!
And let me know when your gum
is ready for blowing bubbles!"

The sound of chewing became
louder and louder.

several

Then several children called out,
"I think my gum is ready!"

Everyone became quiet.
The children put their gum into the
bubble maker, and Harvey turned it on.

In a minute, they saw a very small
bubble appear.
"Ha! A baby could blow a
bubble bigger than that!" said Al.

appear

Nancy made a face and said,
"Besides, that's a strange shape for
a bubble."

strange

43

"A bubble should be round!"

round

45

"Well, no use hanging around here,"
said Al.
The crowd turned to go.

"Wait! Give it time to work!"
said Harvey's father.

Harvey hit the bubble maker a
few times and said,
"Come on! Get going!"

47

The bubble maker burped.
Then it began to sound as though
it was working very hard.
"I wonder what it's doing,"
said Harvey's mother.

"It's blowing!" shouted Al.
"And the bubble is getting bigger!"
People held their breath as they
watched the size of the bubble increase.

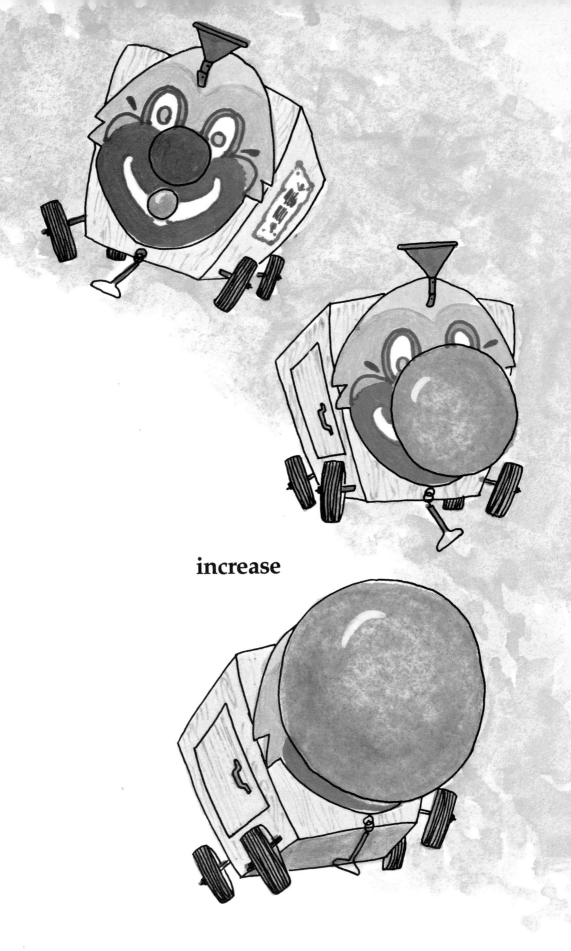

increase

49

"That must be the biggest
bubble gum bubble in the world!"
yelled Nancy.
"Harvey will be famous!"

The crowd almost swallowed their gum.

famous

And still the bubble kept growing.
Harvey was afraid that it would break.
So he tied it off with string and
gave it to his little sister.
The bubble was so light that it
stayed up in the air like a balloon.

The crowd ran toward the
bubble maker and filled
it full of bubble gum.

The bubble maker began
to produce one bubble after another.
Harvey tied them off and gave them
out as fast as he could.

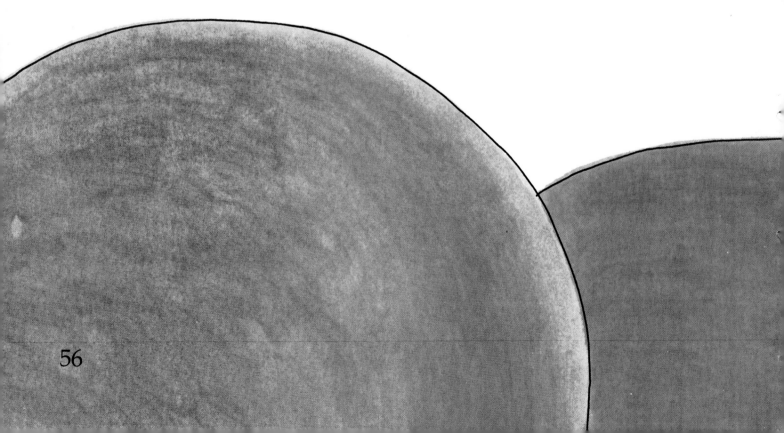

produce

Al pointed to a bubble that was
very big and round.
He said, "Hey, that's a good one!
But mine is better!"

Everyone with a bubble held it up to
see which was the best of all.

better

good

best

59

Harvey smiled.
"Now is the time to press the
double bubble button," he thought.
As soon as he did, the bubble maker
began to produce great big double
bubble gum bubbles!

double

61

They were the biggest bubble gum
bubbles of all.
The crowd went wild trying to get them.
The double bubbles were so big that
they carried people up off the ground.

Soon Harvey's family and all of the
neighbors were sailing happily above
the trees.
Harvey took hold of the last double
bubble and felt himself being
pulled high into the air.

As he sailed above the tree tops,
he dreamed about the next bubble
maker that he was going to build.
The new bubble maker would blow
great big bubble gum bubbles too.
But they would be great big square
bubble gum bubbles—
the first square bubble gum bubbles
in the world!

square

The Smallest Monster

Once there were many monsters who
lived on a mountain.
Sometimes they were mean and
played tricks on each other.
But most of the time,
they were pleasant and had fun.

pleasant

More than anything else,
they loved to drive their
monstercycles.

They raced each other up and
down the mountain every day.

As soon as they were born, the
monsters grew very quickly.
By the time they were ten years old,
they were really big—
as big as they were ever going to be.
So on their tenth birthdays, they
were given monstercycles.
And the older monsters allowed them
to race for the first time.

allowed

One day another baby monster was born on
the mountain.
He was the same type of monster as
all the others.
He had green skin, a red nose, one tooth,
twelve toes, and lots of hair.
His mother and father thought he
was beautiful!

type

73

The other monsters thought he was
beautiful too.
But they noticed that he was
very, very small—even for a baby.
So they called him The Smallest Monster.

noticed

Almost ten years went by.
The Smallest Monster was very happy.
He played monster games with his friends.
And he watched the older
monsters race their monstercycles.

Oh, how The Smallest Monster wanted a
monstercycle of his own!
Having one was his greatest desire.
But he was almost ten years old.
And he was still very small.
And he would not grow any more.
And the monstercycles were much too
big for him to drive.
So he knew that he would never,
ever get one for his birthday.
And that was that.

desire

As The Smallest Monster's birthday
came closer and closer,
he became less and less happy.
He spent more and more time in his room.
He just sat and looked out the window.

less

less

A few days before his birthday,
he saw a group of his friends going by on
their monstercycles.
They were on their way to a big race.

group

The Smallest Monster could not
stand it any longer.
He came out of his room screaming at
his mother and father.

"I don't care if I am too small to
drive a monstercycle!
I want one anyway!
And I demand that you get me one for
my birthday!"

Then The Smallest Monster broke into
tears and ran back into his room.

demand

The Smallest Monster's friends
knew how unhappy he was.
Even though they were monsters,
they felt sorry for him.

"I think we should give The
Smallest Monster a really great
birthday party!" said one of them.

"We agree!" said the others.
Then they got the
older monsters to help them.

agree

87

First The Two Smartest Monsters
got together to make a plan for the party.

plan

When the plan was complete,
all of the monsters went to work.
They made birthday hats and
blew up balloons.
They baked a birthday cake and
made ice cream.

complete

They gathered flowers to put on
the party table.

gathered

93

And on top of the mountain,
they removed the big rocks.
The monsters wanted a lot of
space for dancing and playing.

space

All of The Smallest Monster's friends
had made gifts for him.
They knew they should not tell him what
they had made, and they didn't.
But it was hard for them to
control themselves.

control

On The Smallest Monster's birthday,
a group of monsters went to his house.
They knocked on his door and called,
"Hurry up! It's time for the party!"

"I won't come out!" said a voice from
inside the house.
"If I can't have a monstercycle,
I don't want a party!"

The Smallest Monster's mother and
father had to lift him from his
bed and carry him outside.

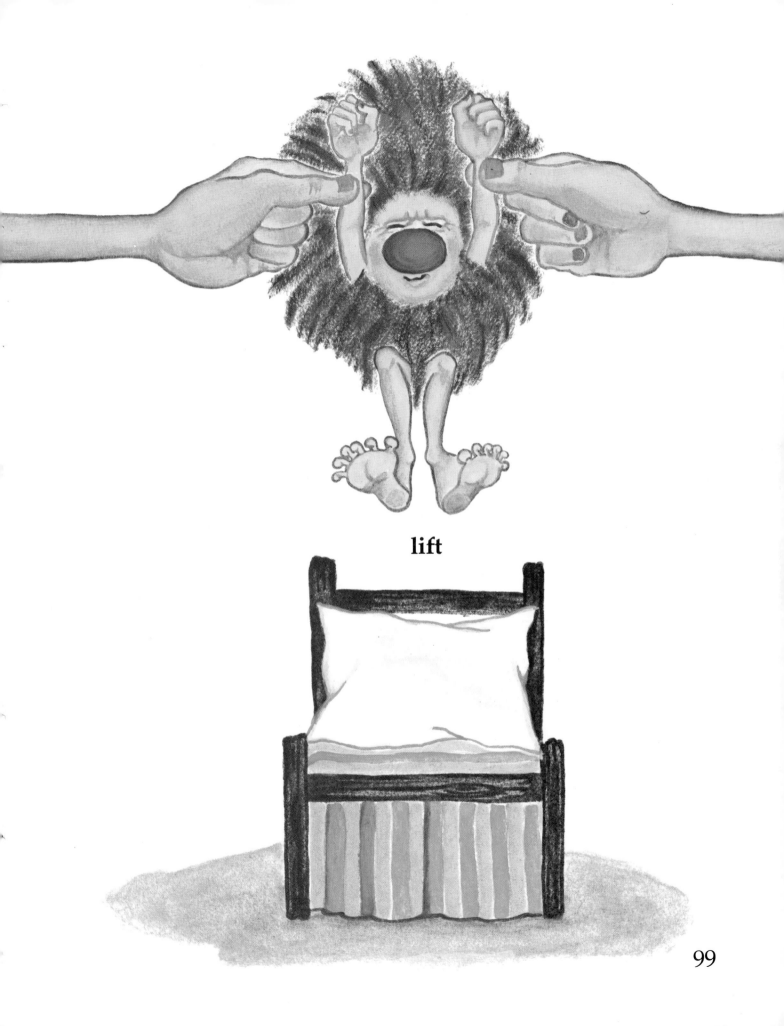

lift

The Smallest Monster was very angry.
His eyes were narrow, and he
showed his tooth and growled.
"That's enough!" said his mother.
"Everyone has worked hard on this
party, and you are going to be there!"

100

The Smallest Monster's father took him by
the hand and started up the mountain.
The other monsters followed.

When everyone got to the top of
the mountain, the party began.
The monsters had a great
time dancing to the music of the
monster band.

Even The Smallest Monster couldn't
help tapping his toes to the music.

After they had danced awhile,
the monsters played games.
Then it was time to eat.
The Hungriest Monster ran to
get the food.
There were cheers when he brought
out a great big chocolate cake.

The Hungriest Monster wanted to
eat the whole thing himself.
Of course, he never could have
gotten away with it.
So he cut a piece for everyone.
The biggest piece went
to The Smallest Monster.

There were more cheers when
The Hungriest Monster brought out a
great big block of rainbow ice cream.

divided

The other monsters watched him closely as
he divided it into squares.

The Two-headed Monster growled and
growled about his share.
Each head wanted its own plate of
cake and ice cream.

share

109

When everyone had eaten,
The Smallest Monster began to open
his presents.
By that time, he looked quite pleasant.
The first box that he opened
contained an eye to put on his forehead.

contained

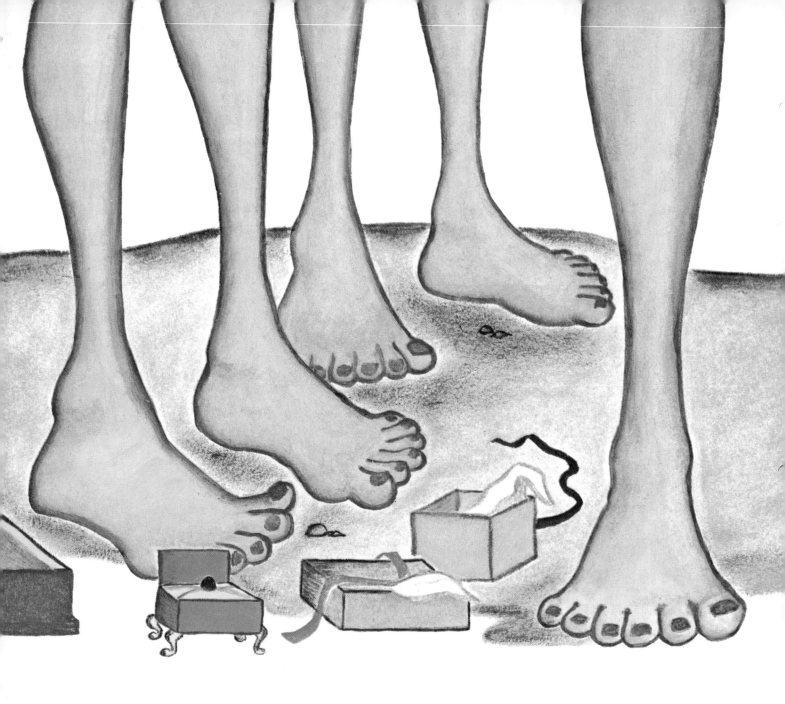

The second box contained a
wart to put on his nose.
The Smallest Monster opened a
few more gifts.

believed

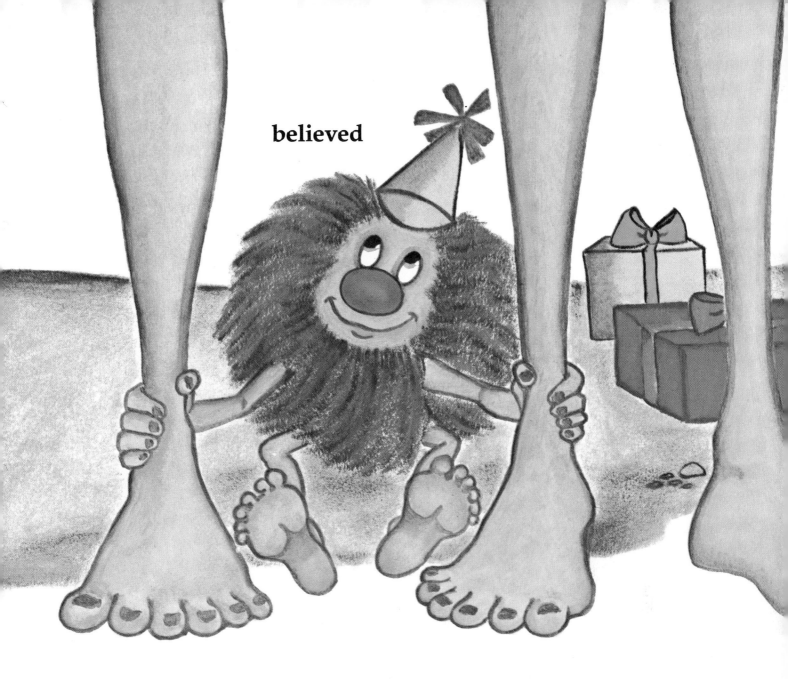

He liked them all.
And he believed that everyone
was trying to make him happy.

But he felt sad when he looked at
the boxes that were left.
He doubted that any one of them was
large enough to contain a monstercycle.

After he had opened his last gift,
The Smallest Monster heard a sound that
he had heard many times.
The sound was a loud roar, and it was
getting louder and louder.

doubted

Someone was coming up the mountain on
a monstercycle!
When the driver reached the top of
the mountain, the monsters shouted happily.

reached

It was the most beautiful
bright yellow monstercycle that The
Smallest Monster had ever seen.
But even more important, it was a
special size that was just right for him!

special

The Smallest Monster almost fell over.
He had to hold onto his mother and
father for support.
He looked up at them and whispered,
"Where did you get it?"

support

121

"From The Very Best Monstercycle Builder,"
said his father.
"No one else could make it."

"Each little monstercycle part had
to be made by hand," explained his mother.

The Smallest Monster jumped on
his monstercycle.
He threw up his arms and shouted,
"Thank you, thank you, thank you!"

Someone yelled, "Give it a try!"
Before anyone could say another word,
The Smallest Monster went
roaring down the mountain.

When he returned, he was like a
different monster.
He even looked a little bit taller.

returned

It was getting dark.
The monsters made a big fire.
Then they formed a
circle around The Smallest Monster and
sang the birthday song.

126

formed

"Happy Birthday to you!
Happy Birthday to you!
You look like a monster!
And you drive like one too!"